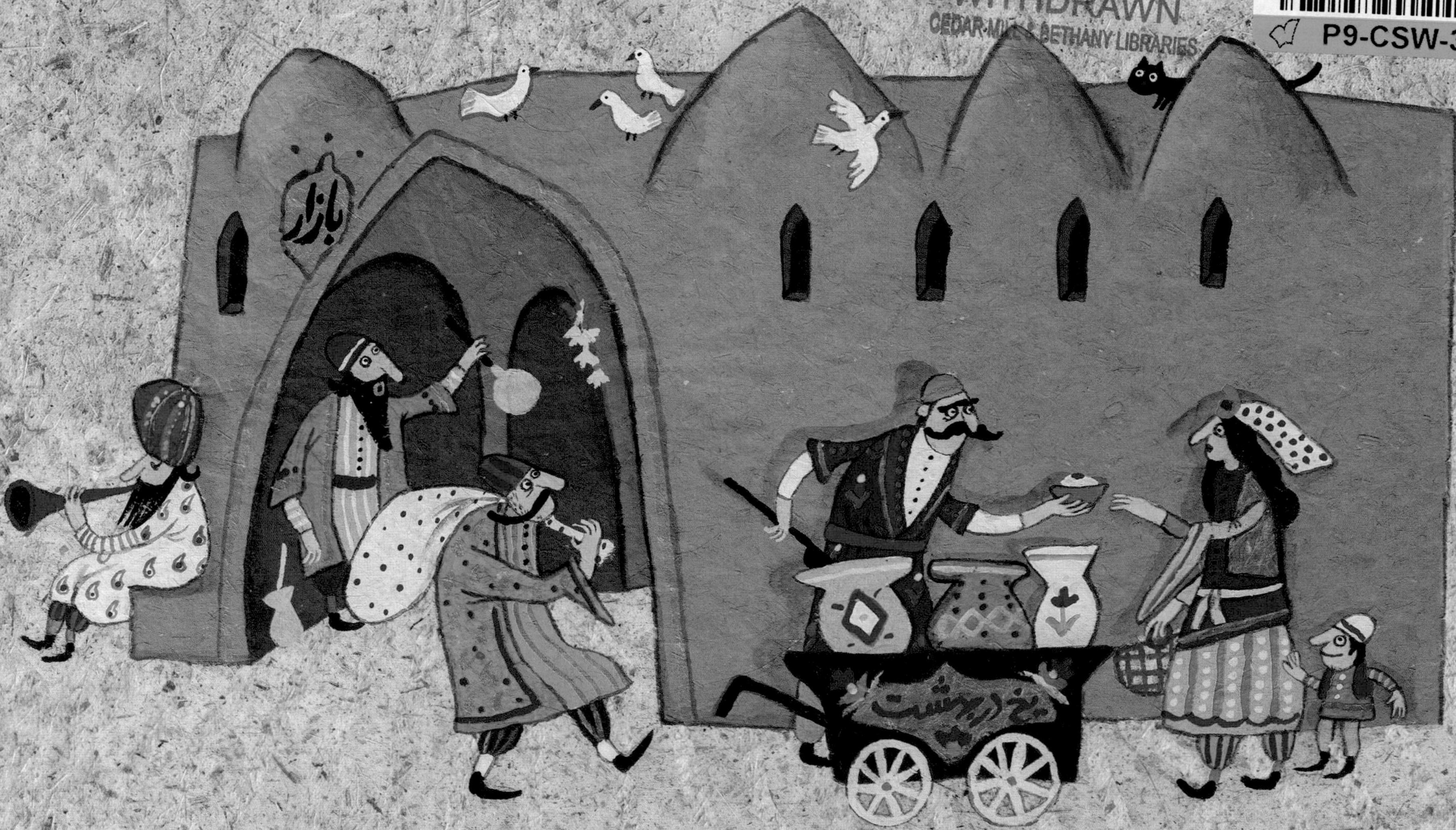
بازار

First published in the United States, Great Britain,
Canada, Australia, and New Zealand in 2014 by
NorthSouth Books, Inc., an imprint of
NordSüd Verlag AG, CH-8005 Zürich, Switzerland.

Distributed in the United States
by NorthSouth Books Inc., New York 10016.
Library of Congress
Cataloging-in-Publication Data is available.
ISBN: 978-0-7358-4171-0
Printed in China by Leo Paper Products Ltd.,
Kowloon Bay, Hong Kong, February 2014.
1 3 5 7 9 • 10 8 6 4 2
www.northsouth.com

Two Parrots

by Rashin

Inspired by a Tale from Rumi

North
South

To all kids who love birds
—Rashin

ONCE UPON A TIME, in Persia, there was a merchant who traveled the world for his business.

On one of his journeys to India,
he received a beautiful parrot as
a gift from a friend.

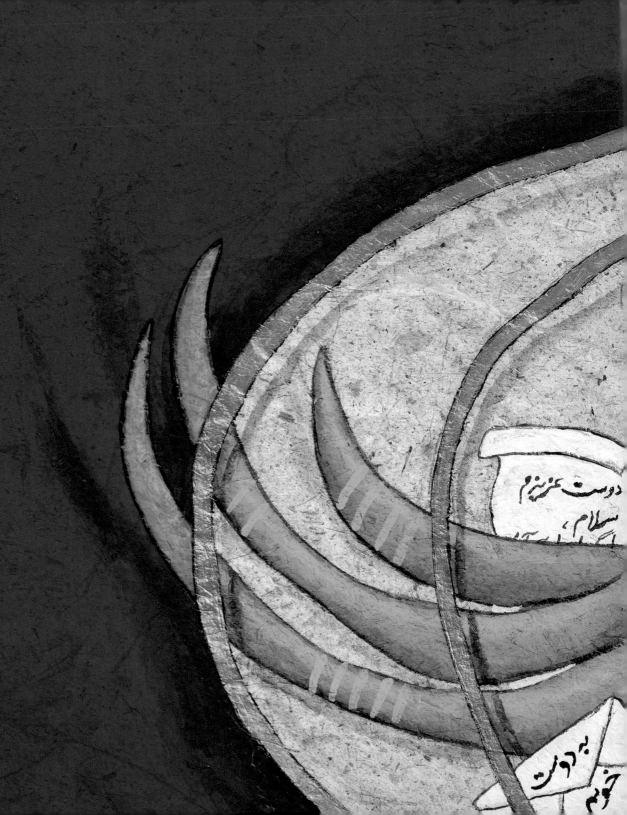

He loved the pretty bird with
all his heart and happily took
him home and put him in a
shiny golden cage.

Days passed, but no matter
how much the merchant cared
for his parrot, the colorful bird
seemed sad.

One day the merchant had to travel to India again. Being a generous man, he asked his servants what he could bring back as a gift. Each asked for something special, and the merchant gave each his promise.

"What present would you like me to bring from India?" the merchant asked his parrot.

"When you see the parrots of India, look for my friend and tell him all about me. Tell him that I would love to see him, but I can't because I live in a cage," the parrot answered.

The merchant loved his parrot so much that
he couldn't imagine letting him out of the cage
for fear of losing him, but he promised to deliver
the message and then left to go on his trip.

At the very end of his visit to
India, the merchant went to a big
garden full of parrots. He found
his parrot's friend and repeated his
parrot's exact words. All the birds
listened to him carefully.

But the moment he finished the last sentence, his parrot's friend began to tremble and fell down dead. The merchant couldn't believe his eyes.

"How can I tell this sad news to my parrot?"

A few days later, the merchant arrived home. He quickly gave all his servants their presents. Then he went to his parrot.

"Did you give my
message to my friend?"
his parrot asked him happily.
   "Yes . . . but I regret what I
did," said the merchant.
   "Why should you feel sorry?"
asked the parrot.

The merchant told him the whole
story. The moment he finished, his
parrot trembled and fell down dead,
just like the parrot in India.

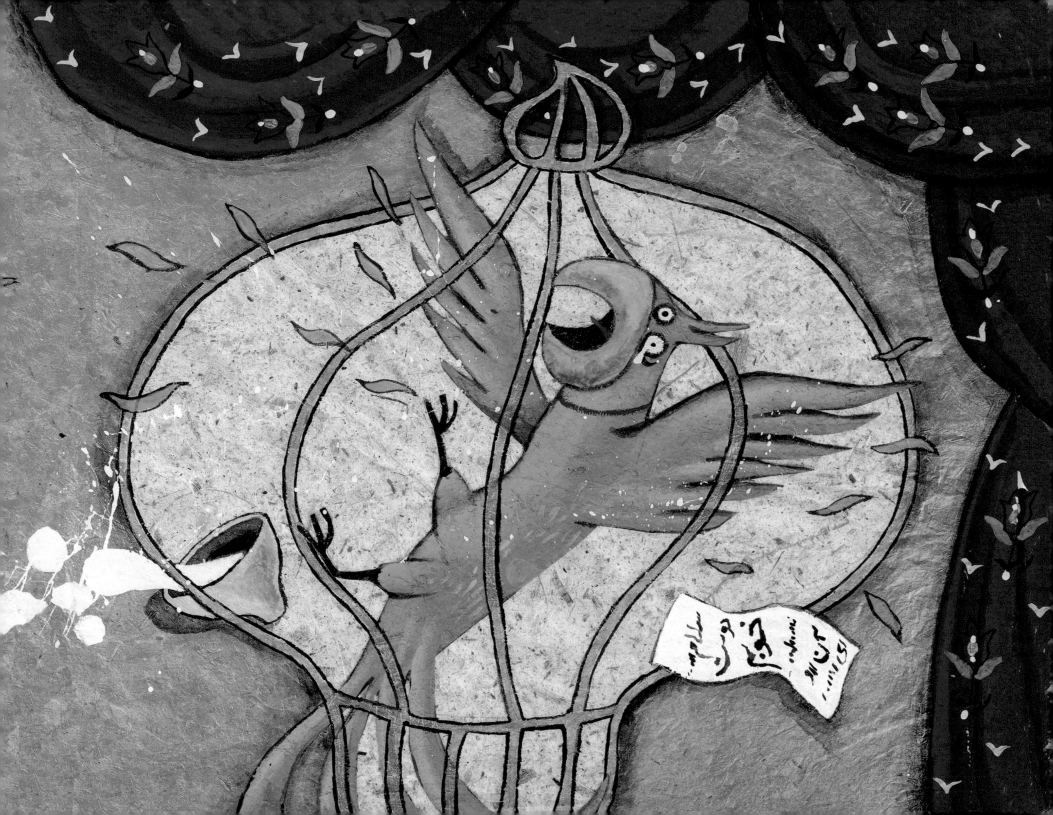

The merchant was shocked. "What happened to you, my sweet bird? Why did you die?" he said as tears trickled down his face. But as he held the bird in his arms . . .

. . . his parrot flew out of his hands and escaped through an open window into the garden.

"My sweet bird, tell me what's going on. Why are you acting like this?" the merchant asked the parrot.

"This is the trick that my friend taught me. He showed me that I could only regain my freedom by playing dead.

"You have always been a nice master to me, but I am a bird and wish to be free. I don't want to spend my whole life in a cage," said the parrot.

The merchant thought for a while and then said, "You're right. Freedom is more important than food and water and all the wealth in the world. You taught me a lesson I will never forget. You are welcome to live in my garden anytime," said the merchant.

The pretty parrot was happy to hear these words from the generous merchant but flew away.

A few days later the parrot came back to the merchant's garden with his good friend. And the merchant was happy to have the company of two beautiful parrots occasionally.

Rumi

Jalāl ad-Dīn Muhammad Balkhī, also known as Jalāl ad-Dīn Muhammad Rūmī, or simply as Rumi, (September 30, 1207–December 17, 1273) was a thirteenth-century Persian poet, theologian, and Sufi mystic. His poetry is revered around the world. He is currently considered to be the "most popular poet in America." His words of wisdom and spirituality are just as pertinent now as they were in his time.

Rashin

Rashin Kheiriyeh, born in Iran in 1979, is one of the most outstanding young Iranian illustrators and animation directors working today—having illustrated more than forty-five books for children and winning numerous awards, including the prestigious Golden Apple Award at the Biennial of Illustration Bratislava (BIB), Slovakia in 2011. Luckily for us, Rashin now lives in America. NorthSouth Books is thrilled to introduce her unique and vibrant work to readers in the Western world. *Two Parrots* is her first book published in the United States.